ROLLING REALITY

Being in flux

By

J. J. BHATT

ISBN:

9798586282408

Title:

ROLLING REALITY:
Being in the flux

Author:

J.J. Bhatt

Published and Distributed by Amazon and

Kindle worldwide.

This book is manufactured in the United States of America.

PREFACE

ROLLING REALITY: *Being in flux* is an examination of humanity's continual state of change, especially in this terrific twenty-first century. It is increasingly becoming clear, modern man is involuntarily caught by the ever explosive super-techs, the rising fear of climate change, nukes and the overall concern for children's future. All these dynamics as mentioned is forcing him to live in a world where there is limited choice al la freedom. Albeit threatening his very privacy, dignity and honor. It is time, he takes stand and fights for his self-esteem and freedom with an eye on a hopeful future for his children."

J.J. Bhatt

CONTENTS

Will to
Win

What if
Human is
Reduced to a
Conceptual
Experience
In the end

Will that
Erode all
Falsities to
Clear the
Way forward
Or what

He's been
Facing
Contradictions,
Paradoxes while
Seeking for
His meaning

Against
All odds,
Let him remain
Calm and be
A determined will
To the end...

Mission

Meaning of
Total reality
Seems
Locked-into the
Moral being only

There is
No give or take
There is only
Necessity to know
The inner core

Intelligent
Being exists
To inspire
Million others

Let him
Glow forever
To sustain
Integrity of his
Blessed soul...

Pivot

Wonder,
How
Relevant is
His individual
Liberty in the
Modern world

It's a big
Question
It's a big
Concern
To be
Raised today

How long
Before AI's
Take charge
I mean,
How long
Before his
Freedom is
No more

Wonder
How sure is
Human of
His awareness
I mean,
How much
He cares for
His self-esteem
Today!

Declaration

Why
Be locked
Into a finite
Time
When we're
The reality
Of this
Eternal clock

We're
Evolving souls
Yes,
We're inspiring
Experience and
We're
Soaring higher
And higher even
Higher than the
Holy heavens

We're
The truth of
All-That Is
Let it be our
Noble Mission
To keep rolling...

My
Essence

I am
A small
Drop into this
Living thinking
Reality that
I've come to
Know

Whatever
It may be,
Seems I must
Face the forces
Of good and evil,
Love and hate...
Life and death
All consequences
To be human,
Indeed

'Am
A speck that's
Dragging along
With a stubborn
Insatiable curiosity
To know my truth

Oh
Yes 'am just
A petite spark
Trying to save
My dignity and
Self-respect...

Our Story

Ancient folks
Saw meaning into
The heavenly stars,
And began worshipping
The Sun God and many
More

In time,
As complexity of
Life increased
So did challenges
To live well

But bursts of
Tribal warfares
Began and
Imposing their
Will on one
Another to govern

Sadly the story
Hasn't changed
Since then
As we
Keep fighting
In the name of
Different
Gods, national prides,
Money, arrogance,
Greed and much more...

Necessity

Life is
But a brief
Experience

Yet
Clarity and
Credibility
Are necessity
To sustain it
Forever

Let's
Understand,
"What's the
Purpose
To exist"

Let's
Not be docile
Let's just
Roll the ball
And spark
The Moral Self
Where our real
Freedom waits...

The
Disease

Let's
Identify
The disease
First

Oh yes,
It's the
Ever sticky
Ignorance;
Nourishing
Arrogance and
Dogmatic claims
Also

Is it
The wrath of
Divinity that is the
Reason or what?
Is it
The fear of
Hell perhaps or
Death as always!

The
Quest

Why
Treasure of
Truthfulness is
Hidden from us
For so long

Where is
That
Intelligent
Being and
Why
Is he not on
The scene

Where is
That human
With deep
Love and hope
Who cares for
Many,
But nowhere
To be seen...

In
Slumber

What
If we are
Nothing but
Living off a
Borrowed
Old habits
Simply

What if
False
Narratives
Stole our
Ideals
Over the
Time only

What if
We've
Missed Truth
In this confined
Sphere of
Tribal mindset
Simply!

Nonchalant

In the best
Civilized times,
There were
Slaves and
Women
Who yearned
For their equal
Freedom, but didn't
Materialized

Kings and
Nobility and
Their armies
Thought had
The Divinely
Permission
To rule, to war
And to kill many,
But they vanished
For good

Then
Emerged the
Servants of God
To rule million minds
And kept them under
Their grip for a long

Well
Here we're
Today being
Challenged by the
"Techno-Lords"
Once again...

Info Age

We freely
Express
Ideas and
Opinions so
Easily then
Ever before

Well with
Good also
Spills badly
So we live
In the age of
Mass confusion,
As well

Seems
We're
Not on the
Right track for
There is so much
Corrupt info in the
Cyber place

Wonder,
How shall we
Reset our sanity
And gain clarity
In such a turmoil of
Our time...

Oneness

We know
The world via
Perceptions,
Intuitions and
Memories and
Much more

Our
Point of view
Defines
The rational
Expression
What it is
'Now"

Yes,
We're the
Riders running
Through the
Foggy nights and
Looking for a
Bright light

We're
Giant candors
Soaring
High and above
Where we're
The awakened
Conscience of
'All-There Is'
Indeed to grasp ...

Mental
Grip!

Where
Induction
Takes us from
Specific to general,
Deduction dives from
Universal to specific

Each
A tool of thinking
Lets us penetrate
Deep shaft of the
Mystery that is
Been teasing for a
Long

What if
We resolve
All queries via
The realm of
Quantum
That is powered
By uncertainty,
Randomness and
Many counter-
Intuitive things!

Knuckle-head

We're
Being buried
Beneath our
Linguistic
Mess

Yes to the
Fallacies of
Ambiguity of
Equivocation to
Name the one

Wonder
How
In the world
We can
Go forward
In the name of
Our Truth

If
We can't clarify
What we think,
What we read
And communicate
Among ourselves?

Gauntlet

Foremost
Challenge of
Modern man is
How to regain
His
Genuine being

I mean,
What
He used to be
Before
The assault of
Rapid techno-
Change

Let him
Rethink
Before
It's too late

Let him
Atleast
Reconsider,
'Simplicity 'and
'Humanity' in
The same box...

Funny
Reality

Life
Though
Ornamented
With beauty
And Truth,
Alas has its
Despair as well

Love
Though
So sweet, yet
At times it's
An ugly game

Ambition
Though
Inspiring to
One,
At times
So damning
To the whole...

Blinkers

Knowing
This wounded
Human,
His
Dignity is a
Necessity
Every time

That is
Where he
Must take
The first
Humble step
To become
Better than
Before

Knowing
The cause
Of his
Suffering,
It's a
Necessity he
Must reset life
On the right track...

Miracle,
Not Yet

Being
Always an
Inquisitive mind
Asking to know
Every twist and
Turn of his
Existence at
All times

Noble is
The being
Himself yet
Unable to meet
His potential

He's
A perplexed
Creative state
And always
Asking to be
Fearless at
All times

Why is
He then so
Hesitant to
Go beyond his
Constraints!

Incredible

Amazingly
Men's
Universe is
But an endless
Riddles,
Possibilities and
Uncertainties

And in such
A milieu of
Doubts and
Debates...he's
Simply spinning
Around to know
His meaning

Existence
What a
Sacred time
To test the depth
Of his rational
Insight

Let him
Wither through
Chaos,
Contradictions
And paradoxes to
Discover his
Freedom...

Confession

So long
'Am on a
Right path
I shall continue
To be
A flashing light
Of my point of
View

Of course,
It's a journey
Of either/or,
Right or wrong
Good or otherwise

Oh yes,
This is the
Only trail where
I am the
Sole expression
Of my point of
View...

Beware

One day
We shall all
Turn into a
Gray powder
Called, "Urn"

I mean,
We shall
Returned to
Mother Earth
May be
To nourish
A new plant or
Something else

Beyond
Cacophony of
The daily struggle,
There is life
To be lived and
Lived well

There is
A moral path
To follow... to be
Worthy of our
Births...

Self
Critique

Why
Don't we
Understand,
"Human soul
Is our pure
Consciousness"

I mean,
Have we
Ever asked,
"Where is the
Genuine Beauty
And Truth of
My inner being"

Did we
Even care to
Grasp,
"Essence of
Being is timeless
And fear of death
Mustn't be ever"

Have we
Ever probed,
'What is the
Meaning of our
Existence in its
Fullest sense!"

Get off
The Cave

In the
Beginning,
Folks thought,
Everything was
Manifest of
Only One

Much later
Emerged
Madness of
Geographic
Multi-gods

And then
The world was
Thrown into
Chaos and many
Wars

Sadly
Today,
Our kind is
Still divided
And not free
From all that
Dated zealotry
Claims...

Inquisitive

What
Exists and
How we know
Is a big question
To probe

While into
The arena of
Inquiry
There are
Some
Contradictions
And paradoxes
We shall always
Encountered
For we're not
There yet

Oh yes,
We exist to
Widen the
Interpretation
Of our knowledge
And experience

That seems
To be
The essence
Of our journey
Through life
While we got
This last chance...

Contextual

Being
A magical
Link between
Two opposites:
Temporal and
Eternal
Despair and
Hope
Love and hate
And
Many more

Yet he's
Unable
To tie all the
Opposites in
Unity with his
Corrupt state of
Mind

It seems
He has million
Miles to go before
Entering the temple
Called,
" The Beauty Truth."

Endeavor

What if
The world is
Nothing but
Verily an
Expression of
Moral Will

I mean,
Where every
Single
Soul must
Meet his/her
Social call

Will it
Still fulfill the
Set noble goal to
The end or what!

Duty
Call

To be is
To be good
Over a prolong
Period of time

To be is
To take a
Right stand
To illumined the
Young braves

To be is
To sustain
Social stability
And dignity of
All humans over a
Prolong period of
Time...

Walk the Walk

Let us
Get off the
Myopic sphere
And let the Self be
At the center of
Ethical call

Let us
Experience
The open world of
Love and laugher
For life is so brief
To be despaired

Let us
Just plunge into
The realm of
Beauty and truth
To discover, "Who
We are at the core"

Let us
Just walk the
Walk and not talk
Anymore.

Force
One

To reckon,
Life is
Mercurial and
And shortened
By every ticking
Sound of the very
Old clock

Yes,
The goal is
To know,
"We're born
To know our
Truth"

That is
How we must
Direct the
Journey ahead
And that's the
Only
Choice we got,
Today...

Star
Child

So
What
If we are
A speck in the
Totality of this
Mighty and vast
Universe

After all
We're
Everything in it
Whose searching for
A meaning of it all

Yes,
We're
Free to roam
As we wish, to think
Or to imagine
At will

That is
Our true
Freedom and
That's
Our wonderful
Gift indeed...

Sweet Cake

Existence
Is a three
Layered cake:

At the top
There is the
Moral will
In the middle,
A rational drive
And at the
Bottom, a
Constant struggle
To overcome the
False belief

That is how the
Pyramid of deep
Reality is printed on
Every soul but not
In equal degrees
To report

Let's
See how we
Shall make the
Journey from the
Bottom to the top
Worthwhile or not!

Only
Way

Let
Simplicity
Be the first
Principle

Let
Reason
Be the
Strength

And
Don't let
Compassion
Go off the
Track

Don't let
The journey
Go off
The ramp

Don't let
Hope
Slip off the
Moral Self.

The Force

Fearless
HARSHA
Inspired
His siblings
To go beyond

To seek
Opportunity
When the storm is
Knocking off all
The big dreams

He asked,
To strive for
Understanding
When
Trapped into a
Dark realm of
Doubts

He insisted
To be a
Determined will
When the whole
World says, "Nay"

Harsha
What an
Immortal force
Challenging,
"To stand tall
Against
All odds and still
Succeed in the end."

Take
Charge

A coin
Tossed into
The air got
Two sides:
Freedom and
Responsibility
Alright

While
Airborne,
The two faces
Are well balanced
And all is uncertain,
But so calm

Once it hits
The floor
Only one side
Is shown to
The world

If
Every coin
Got two sides,
Why ignore
The other side of
Freedom always!

Triumphant

What if
We're verily
Metaphysical
Experience while
Riding through this
Ephemeral empirical
Realm

Will it
Still thrill us
To the great
Beyond,
I mean
To perplexity,
Beauty and
Truth

Let the
Inner force,
"Consciousness"
Link us with all
Its rhythm and
Meaning at once

Let the
Freewill fire-up
New ideas, new
Vision and ever
So new quests...

Ascension

Albeit
"I"
A speck into
This revolving
Reality where
Am the
Temporary
Claim only

As I keep
Ascending
Far and above
"I" gain
Petite insight that
I'd not known

Still 'am
Happy to be in
This complexity
That is so
Challenging
Every minute...

Pre-Requisite

To take a
Bold stand
To meet the
Modern
Demand to
Go smooth
On the ride

And
To build a
Better world
Than ever
Before

To
Experience
Harmony in
This violence
And chaos

Let's begin
With
Tolerance and
Understanding
As the first step...

Together

Our
Creative
Gift
Shall take us
Million miles
Away from
The present
Terrible plight

Let us
First
Unshackle
From the
Pseudo
Tribal-claims

Let us
Be
One mighty
Force of the
History
In-making...

Eternal
Issue

Awareness
Still a
Conceptual
Consequence of
The mind

Whatever
Its source,
Let it be
The first step

And
I wonder,
"Why
Truth still
Keeps swinging
Between stubborn
Conceptuality and
Beyond!"

Spirit
Said

Spirit
Said,
"I am
Never born,
Therefore
I am
Forever"

"What do
You mean?"
The body
Snapped

The spirit
Explained,
"I am
Temporal here
But eternal in
The totality of
All that is"

"So!"

"Hey
Ignorant one
That's how
How I roll you
From known
To the Unknown
Over and again..."

Illumined

How to
Measure
My meaning
When
I've to walk
Alone this
Rough terrain

How to
Make it right,
When I got
No disciplined
Habits to keep
The road straight

I even
Tried to
Stay alert and
Calm, but again
I keep walking
Alone through the
Rough terrain for
Reason I don't
Understand...

To Be

Only
Action
Shall win
Dignity and
Honor in time

Let's
Demystify
Divinity and
All fairy tales
And learn to
Walk on a
Right track

Yes,
Let's keep
Moving toward
A place where
We shall be
Awakened spirits
For the first time...

Happy
Days

To
Young
Braves:

Keep the
Journey going
'Til you got the
Reward in time

Be sure to
Make life
Relevant
While you got
This chance

Be
Disciplined
And
Be inspired
To fulfill
Your dreams
Before it's too
Late...

Social Call

Let
Each
Extend
Friendship to
Another

Let's
Listen to
To one another
While we're
Sailing through
The rough sea

Let's
Gain basic
Understanding
For the children's
Sake...

Beautiful

Each is
Good and evil
At the
Same time

For we're
Responsible
For our thoughts,
Words and deeds

It's
Paramount
We transcend
Present state
And begin
Knocking doors
Of our inner being

Remember,
We're the
Consequence
Of our thoughts,
Words and deeds
Before kissing the
Noble death...

Duty
Call

Across
The globe
Folks keep
Wondering,
"What's
Happening in
Their world"

Across
The globe
They're asking,
"Why there is so
Much corruption
In the world"

Even
Young are
Concerned,
"What is their
Future in this
Uncertain world "

But the
Good folks
Forget to ask,
"How should I be
An asset to my
Community today?"

Distillation

Intelligent
Being though
A tiny speck in
The universe

Can be
Bold to
Comprehend
Myriad
Riddles with his
Rational insight

Being
Who's a
Supreme
Potential
To actualize
His infinite
Possibilities
Any time
Wants

But don't
Let him
Undermine his
Will to act soon...

Storm

Traditional
Belief
Taught him to
Fill life with
God's will and
To live for the
Final Judgment
Till the end

All
Divinely
Teachings
Geared to keep
Him on a right
Path

Well, the
Deterministic
Belief robes him
Of his freewill and
Disturbing his moral
Soul every time

Out of fear
Of the Unknown
He keeps begging
For 'Forgiveness'
While disturbing his
Rational instinct
Every time...

Holier Than Thou!

As time
Changed so did
Brands of God:
Once
There were
Rha, Marduk and
Zeus and in time
They faded away
From the religio-
Memory of man

Later
New Gods
Popped-up in
Different tribes
Across the world
And new claims
Kept on emerging
On the scene

Each
Branded Divine
Painted the
Canvas of humanity
In myopia and
Bloody red; eroding
Moral strength
Most everywhere...

Zigzag
Way

What if
Reality is a
Consequence
Of our solipsist
Assumption

What if
All is merely a
Conceptual play
To hide ignorance
Or whatever

Why
Locked onto
"Doubts &
Debates"
When bridge to
The Unknown is
So well linked...

Carousal

It's the
Same old saga
Of every civilized
Society

When
Middle class
Is heavily taxed
And poor neglected
That's when
Good life ends;
Benefiting few
In control

Eventually
Good folks
Loses grip over
Their patience
And the
Consequence,
"Great Tragedy
Of the commons"

So there
Emerges cry for
Big Change and
A new beginning
Keeps the cycle
Going once again...

Janus

What's
The point
In reading
History if it
Keeps
Repeating
Now and then

What's the
Value of faith
If it empowers
To kill in His
Name

What's
The meaning of
Freedom when
Failing to meet
The basic
Moral principle

What's the
Point in
Asking for
Godly
Forgiveness,
When one
Can't offer the
Same to
His fellow man...

Cheer-up

Let's
Dance in
The sunshine,
Yes
In this hour of
Our great joy

Hey folks
Let's sing
And sing loud
To keep
Love flowing
As ever

No need
Saying,
"Sorry"
No need
Declaring,
"I don't care"

Let's just
Hold hands
And keep the
Dream going,
Going...going
So well

Yes folks,
Let's sing the
Song louder than
Ever, "Yes we do
Care, we do care...
We do care always..."

Clarity

Time to
Suspend all
Crazy whims
Time to roll-up
The sleeves

No point
In fighting for
Different brands
When HE is the
Only ONE

No need
To repent, no
Need to complain
No need to blame
Others
Just drop the
Absurd claim
And move on

Let us
Keep the
Journey going
With a meaning
For we live on a
Borrowed time
Only...

Passage

While
We're on
The road to
Self-Knowing,
Let us be Aware:

We're
Born to
Resolve all
Conceptual
Errors to clarify
Our Truth

We're
Not afraid
To explore all
Possibilities to
Reach the set
Goal

We're
Confident of
Our moral will
While we're on
This road to the
Self-Knowing
As an end goal...

Challenge

Belief in
Divine was a
A sudden burst
Of epiphany

It was
Kindled by a
Few awakened
Spirits who
Sought ways
How to journey
Toward light

What a pity,
This simple truth
Lost its meaning
By the false-
Narratives which
Upwelled from the
Fragmented beliefs

Let there
Be only
One universal
Validation,
"Humanity
Above all only"

Bridge

Don't let
The bridge
Keep hanging
Between
Something and
Nothing

Don't
Let the
Chaos rule
Everything
While he's
Struggling

Don't let
Zealots
Claim their
Crazy whims

Don't let
Them
Divide our
Love, hope
And children's
Big dream...

Main
Issue

How
Do we save
Our kind and
The Planet in
The best way
We must

How
Do we
Grasp a
Rational way
To change the
Destructive
Path we've
Been for long

I mean.
How do we
Restore our
Simplicity,
Dignity and
Humanity
At this time...

Prayer

Let us
Meditate,
All That Is
To fulfill our
Long waited
Dream

Let us
Also be aware,
How to keep
Rolling through
This long dark
Tunnel, today

Time
To be embolden
And let's begin
With the song of
Courage

Yes, yes
Let us dare
Walk through
The trail with a
Greater ease today...

Awakening

We live
For many
Dreams and
Then we leave
The world
So soon

Why
We fail to
Know right
From wrong
When we've
The smart brain

Why
Fail to
Think good
When that is the
Necessasity to
Survive and
Succeed

Why
Believe in
False-claims
When truth is
Always, within...

The
Spell

As we
Keep plowing
Through this
Techno-driven,
"Crazy world"

There's a
Growing concern
We've become
Its victims

As we
Remain
Immersed into
This techno-magic
From dusk to dawn
We're losing
Our first-hand
Human connections

We've
Been showered
By the fake-news,
Shallow opines and
Never ending lies
And deceptions
All leading to a silent
Brain injury alright...

Big
Picture

A cosmic
Worm hole,
What a possible
Reality to know

Human
What a
Mercurial
Experience
Who exists a
Moment or two
And he's no more
On the scene

Life
Very dynamic
Yet so brief
Where truth
Is the only light
Challenging
To think beyond
Cosmic worm holes...

Be
Happy

Let's just
Keep moving
With alacrity
And big hope

Let's just
Sing and dance
'Til the goal is
Fulfilled

Let's
Salute to be
Born in
Human form

Let's
Beat this
Existence of
'Trials and errors'
And let's seize the
Best of our time...

Forever

Darling,
I've loved you
For a long

Sweetheart,
Let me say,
"You've been
My dream gal
For whom
Waited so long"

Dear love,
I ask, "Why
Ignore the deep
Feelings that
Are already
Firing-up within"

Darling,
Why not sing
Together our
Sweet song:

If the world
May or may
Not care, but let
Our love be the
Truth forever, yes
Forever, forever...

Salute

Salute
To all great
Minds
Who inspired
The world for
A long time

Salute
To all lovers
For enriching
Human
Experience
To the core

Salute
To all
Enlightened
Souls who
Lifted our
Spirits from
Deep grief to
The immense joy...

Cross-Road

A Wiseman
Went
Every mall
In the town and
Kept asking to
The folks who're
So busy shopping

"Is human a
Spectacular
Gift born to be
Something or
Just a worm who
Exists for nothing?"

They
Blatantly
Ignored him
While attending
Their immediate
Material wants

The wise
Quietly returned
To his home and
Soliloquy,
"I hope folks
Will wake-up, if
They truly desired
Freedom..."

Light &
Dark

Did we
Ever realize,
We're
Two halves,
Good and evil
Always

Did we
Ever realize,
We're
Love and hate
Always

Why
Did we
Not realize,
"We're also
Silently suffering
Beings?"

Do we
Ever realize,
"What's our
Meaning in this
Endless struggle,
Time after time?"

Gist

Existence
What an
Aesthetic
Experience
To give meaning to
Our noble mission

Its
An artistic
Judgment
While on the
Way to be
Beauty & truth

Let us
Strengthened
Our moral essence
Let it be the
Necessary courage
To be the
'Enlightened One'

Let us
Be free to
Pursue to justify
Our entry on this
Incredibly magic
Called,
"The Planet Blue"

Precious

Time
To think
Today for a
Better tomorrow

Time
To inspire
Children with
Good disciplined
Habits today

They're
The future and
They're the light
Of human destiny,
Always

Let's
Give 'em
Love and care
For they're the
Moral gift to
Keep our kind
Alive and well...

Raison D'être

We're
Born to be
Free
From tears
And guilt's

We're
Born to kill
Ignorance with
Reason

We're
Here to
Liberate us
From
Yesterdays
Blunders

Yes, we're
Here to spark
Creativity and
New vision to
Give a meaning to
This magnificent
Existence...

Great
Ride

We
Don't have
Much time left
For the journeys
Too long

Let's
Get on the
Fast track to
Ascend from
Imperfection
To perfection
At this time

Let's drop
This madness
Called, "Tribalism"
And let's open our
Hearts to something
Greater than our
Greed and self-
Interests

Let's act
Smart before
Our sweet dream
Turns into a hellish
Experience...

Journey

What's
An enlightened
Spirit of man
That is the big
Question

Is it the
Apotheosis of
His immutable
Will or what

Is it the
Peak of his
Wisdom or
Something else

Whatever
It may be,
Let it
Light-up
His moral
Thirst while
He's struggling
Through the
Zig zag track...

Dear
Heart

Dear Heart,
"Either
We stay or
We go our
Separate ways"

I say,
"There mustn't
Be a mirage
Between
Our two souls"

Yes,
Sweet heart,
That's the reality
Of love demanding
For a lasting trust

Love is
Our eternal
Link
Love is our
Only breath
Love is
You and I and
I ask you,
To make it up
Once again...

Cosmic Seed

Rejoice,
We're the
Real jewels
In this
Incredibly
Beautiful
Universe

A
Universe
That keeps
Widening
With ever
Unknown
Future

A
Universe
That is
Exploding
With ever
Nova dreams

Let it
Be known,
"We're the
Inheritance of
This magnificent
Vast Universe all
The way to the end..."

Dare

Did we
Ever think,
"We're
The stream of
Consciousness"

Did we
Ever believe,
"We're the
Human-Divine
In equal sense"

Did we
Ever
Dare grasp,
"We're the
Path to our
Own truth"

Did we
Ever have the
Guts to drop all
False narratives
And be the
Enlightened Soul!

Fire
Ball

In the
Pin-drop
Silence of a
Stygian night

A
Person was
Thrown into
A metaphysical
Experience

He was
No longer
Aware of his
Human form,
But
Suspended
Into the brightest
Of all lights

In such a
Blinding brilliance,
He was nothing but
A Nano- fireball
Who's been
Spinning forever...

North Star

When
Caught by the
Barreling storm
No need to panic
But to stay calm
And face it with
Courage

When
Bad times
Knock the door
No need to
Renounce
The world, but
Be a smart player
To play out the
Nasty game to
The end

Don't be
Afraid to swim
Through the
Rhythms of
Right or wrong
For that's the
Daily test of your
Life and time...

Great
Voyage

Through
This precious
Voyage
We keep
Evolving

Don't be
Afraid and
Don't run away
From the world
Of greed and
Anger

Just stand
Bold and
Upgrade the
Habit of moral
Code

I say,
Through
The rhythms
Of Nature,
Keep asking,
"How do I
Lift my humanity
To experience
The real truth
That's pending?"

Be Brave

Let
God seekers
Take one step
Forward and
Let 'em
Go beyond

Life
Mustn't
Be burdened
By the fear of
Any unknown
Either Divine
Or whatever

Let's
Be brave and
Grasp the simple
Riddle with our
Rational strength...

Shooting Stars

Now the
Techno-power
Is the best game
In the town and
There is
No limit to its
Seduction

No need
To regret, but
To seek deeper
Meaning of our
Genuine worth
Let's
Not lose our
Sanity,
Our privacy,
Or our
Freedom

For the
Techno reality
Shall be with us
Forever and there
Is no escape...

Verdict

Chained by
The
Unbearable
Feeling of
Discontent

Being
Seeking
How-to escape
From the world of
Constant turmoil

Yes
He desires to
Run away from
Its chaos and
Never –ending
Quarrels

Let
There be
Awakening
Let there be
A confession of
His piled-up sin...

Pearl

Death
Not an
Option,
But a new
Beginning
For truth in
Essence only

Mysticism,
Just a glimpse,
But never a
Total
Experience

Meditative
State means
He's in union
With the
Moral Self,
While at peace

Being
Neither
Suffering
Nor a crazy
Whim, but a
Pearl of
Total integrity
Of his mind...

Being
Human

Human,
What a
Conscious force
Always driven
By the infinite
Possibilities
Life after life

Human,
What an
Awesome
Creation
Caught into
The abstruse
Sphere of
Myriad riddles
Time after time

Human,
What a lost
Cause who's
Buried by the
Million queries
While onto a
Simple quest of
Mind after mind...

Selfless

There is
Nothing better
Than insisting,
How to be
An asset to
The societal
Needs

There is
Nothing better
Than to be firm
Over cultivating
Mental discipline
First

There is
Nothing
Meaningful
Than be the
Collective
Rational strength
To make it alright

There is
Nothing to be
Afraid in fighting
For harmony, dignity
And peace for
Children's dream...

Sweet
Revenge

Let us
Keep evolving
With full-alacrity
And good strength

Let life
Keep the mission
Going full-speed
With determined
Collective Will

Let us
Not deterred
By the sad news,
Let us be the
Greater cause
With right action

Let life
Keep us rolling
Forward with
Full-alacrity and
Good strength...

Elixir

Oh
This
Wonderful
Gift called,
"Human
Experience"

Let
It be a magic
To resolve all
Our riddles,
At once

Let us
Be happy
Dancers, *par
Excellence*
And let us
Keep dancing
Through the
Thick and thin
With
Full-confidence...

Silence

When
Am in solemn
Silence for days
I belong
To harmony

Who
Holds me
So well in
This throbbing,
But evolving
Universe

That's
Where
My soul is
Healed and
I become,
'Thoughtless
Whole'

Wonder,
If that be
The first
Entry to the
World beyond
Or just a weird
Psychic experience!

Echoes

Folks kept
Crying out
So loud
In the streets
Called,
"Everywhere"

They're asking,
"How do we resolve
The destructive
Issues of our
Time"

Yes,
It's about
Nukes, climate
And the rigid
Beliefs as well

Suddenly,
They heard
Echoes from
Their souls:

*To survive
And to succeed,
Be sure to know,
"How to adapt
To the new reality
Of your time"
Yes,
How to walk
The walk while
On the track...*

Ubiquitous

Let us
Roar and let
Us go far and
Beyond our
Troubles of
Today

Let us
Discover
Truth through
Our
Astoundingly
Beautiful souls

And let it
Be known,
"We're
The genuine
Moral good
At the core"

Fearless

Damn
Right,
We hold on
To our brave
Hearts
To live well

We're
Never say,
Sorry, but
Ready
To forgive
If the cause
Is just right

We're
Never
Perturbed
By the million
Nay Sayers

For we're
The confident
Winners to fly
Higher than
Where we are...

Destination

No
We're
Not seeking
Belief
That divides
Humanity at
The core

We
May be
Accidental
And imperfect
Yet got modicum
Common sense

And that is
Who we are
That is
Where our
Journey must
Begin

Yes to drop
The false narrative
That disturbs
Harmony and peace
Of the mind...

Good
Will

Social
Cohesion
Must evolve
Higher than
Where we are
With individual
Whims of freedom

Our
Collective
Endeavor be
The first
Principle to
Build a world of
Big dream

Let
Reason and
Moral intentions
Be the strength
Behind...

Circle,
"Zero"

Ever
Since the
First spark of
Reckoning,
We began
Wondering,
"What's the
Essence of
Our own being"

And we've
Been probing to
Unfold the secret
Of our truth, yet
We haven't
Corrected the
Blunders from
The past

Wonder,
Why then
Query and
Seek meaning
When
Unable to
Introspect the
Very meaning,
"Who we're at
This turning point?"

Gratitude

Life
What a
Brilliance of
Love and hope
Asking to hit the
North Star always

Consider
Struggles to be
Only a small price
While en route to
The Temple of
Awakening

Keep
Walking
Through the
Swirling winds
Of change and
Don't let it
Disturb your
Will
Don't let it
Throw you
Off the well-set
Trail...

Sealed

After birth
We grow-up
In the company
Of many million
"Yes and no,"
Of course

And we
Hit the gate of
Love where
Countless big
Dreams continue
To roll

In such a
Milieu, we
Keep
Embattling to
Meet our goal

It's a
Struggle
To compete,
To fight and
Even to play
By the rules
While
On the road
Called, "Birth
Kissing Death"

Voice

When a
Child is
Thrown to
The world of
Violence
Called, "War"

Aimlessly
He wonders
Through the
Dark shadows of
Man's cruelty, alright

He cried
Loud enough, but
The deaf world didn't
Hear him at all

Atlast the child
Approached the
'Sacred' place of
Worship and
Declared:

Inspire
Me to be good
Inspire me to be
Sincere and loving
Inspire me to
My truth, if you care...

An Issue

When all
The burden of
Fear and insecurity
Begins to knock
The doors of
Our children's
Big dream

All of a
Sudden, life
Seems ephemeral,
Illusive and
Meaningless at times

What if
All events turn
Into fading memories
And the trail too
Begins disappear
Before
Our tearful eyes

In such
A scenario,
Let us
Rethink and
Ask, "why not
Lift our humanity
Through this timeless
Rhythms and melodies
Of our moral judgment
All the way to the end...

At the
Core

If
Anything
Seems
So constant
In this blessed
Universe

It
Must be the
Pure thought of
Human spirit
Simply

If
Anything
That is
Absolute
Must be the
Mortal fate
Essentially

If
Anything
That is
Unknown
Must be the
Fear of the
Mind only...

Odyssey

After
A journey of
Many millennia,
We've arrived
In this modern
Era of insecurity,
Greed and rampant
Corruptions

In
Other words,
"What did
Accomplish
Thus far
I mean morally?"

Progress
What a long
Experience
Driven by
The endless,
"Trials and errors"
But the
Human nature
Is something else...

Perpetual

Perpetual
Whims
Spinning the
Great Sphere
Called, *The
Big Unknown*

Perpetual
Being can't
Wait to escape
Mediocrity and
Uncertainty at
Once

Perpetual
Being keep
Probing, yet no
Reconciliation
To know his truth

Caveat
Emptor

Thinkers
Declared for
A long time,
"In essence,
Human is either
An intentional or
An accidental
Freak of nature"

Thinkers
Also advised,
"Man shouldn't
Surrender to the
Overly
Materialistic lures"

Thinkers
Even warned,
"If a man
Succumbed
To mindless
Gratifications shall
Erode his dignity,
Privacy and freedom
In the end."

On the
Road

Million
Riddles
And miracles
Scattered all
Over the rough
Terrain called,
"Existence"

Human,
A tiny flicker
Who's struggling
Through its thick
And thin...wishes
To be the winner
Of his adventure
In the end

Oh yes,
For him
Million miles
Yet to go before
He merges with
The truth of his
Genuine being...

Thrust

To grasp
The abstruse
Reality as soon
As we must

To
Grasp unity
With the
Complimentary
Opposites is a
First step

Yes,
To know the
Link between
Thoughts and
Objects we must

To believe
In power within
And how to be a
Determined will
Must be the set goal
That is also the
Equal step always...

It Is

This
Unbounded
Sphere of
Possibilities
Got to be the
Manifest
Being only

That is
Were he's
The judge of
Good and evil,
Love and hate
And many more

Strictly,
It is in the
Realm of
"Pure Silence"
He shall know
The meaning of
All- That-is

Reverence

Our
Gratitude to
Great Spirits
Who left a
Legacy of
Rational and
Ethical habits
For us to be
Inspired always

Yes
It is strictly
For us who're
The owners of
Imperfect state
Of minds

Let us
Remember
Those
Great souls
Who asked
To experience,
"Harmony, beauty
And truth always"

Human To Be

A voice of
Inspiration
Can move
The mighty
Mountain
In a sec

A single
Moral act can
Awake the soul
In an instant

A single
Expression of
Courage can lift
Anyone to the sky
High in no time

A single
Act of
Forgiveness can
Catapulted a person
From hell to the
Heaven in a sec...

Time

Knowing,
Truth
Defines
The essence of
Every being

With such
A moral
Validation
Let us begin the
Journey to fulfill
Our every dream

That be the
Purpose of life
Of every
Intelligent being

Time
Keeps running
And there ain't
Place left to go,
But to stay the
Right path only...

This
Realm

What
We see,
What
We feel and
What we
Understand

At times
Are not the
Same things
Since
We create
Reality in
Our thoughts
Only

What
We intend
And what we
Really are

At times,
Seems
Two different
Things,

Whence
We keep
Bobbing into the
Sea of uncertainty,
Indeed.

Destined

We are
Born to be
Better than
Before

Let us
Dance with
Fresh ideas,
New vision and
Novel ways
Beginning today

Time to be
Inspired and
Time to be
Free from the
Recurring grief...

Reality Check

The holy
Divided us
And in time,
We turned
Violent and
Worthless

Let us
Open our
Rational minds
And be ready to
Change the path
We've been on
For a very long

We're the
Moral power
And let it
Give strength,
How to build
A world of
Meaning

Let us
Together
Learn to do
Something
Good atleast for
The children's sake...

Unfinished

Life,
Love and joy
What a
Wonderful trio
To celebrate

But, don't
Forget to save
Aspiration,
How to measure
Our collective
Worth

Let us
Not be
Nonchalant
On the scene
While heading
To the mountain
Top to know
Our truth...

Awareness

While
On the way
To rewrite
Their
New story

Folks
Asking for
Friendships
And not to be
Strangers
Anymore,
Today

Awakened
Folks
Reminding,
"Ain't time
To complain but
To wake-up and
Begin the walk
To the Temple of
Truth only."

Expedition

I exist
To think,
To motivate
And to explore

I am
My instinct
I am my
Joy and grief

Indeed,
I exist
To seek
My goodwill,
My essence and
My determination
For I hold this
Precious life in
My
Hands once only...

The
Way

What a joy
It is to
Welcome the
Solemn notion,
"Individual Liberty
But with an equal
Responsibility only"

Let it be
Clear, "a good
Society is build
On a balanced
Freedom with
Accountability,
Essentially"

Law,
Order and
Equal justice
Sets the stable
Pillars to keep
The crazy
World civilized
Simply

Creative
Thoughts, great
Arts and futuristic
Vision must keep
Nourishing
Such ideals in
Action forever...

Search

"Where're
We
Heading
Today"

Is there a
Way
Better than
Yesterday

Still
Asking,
"Where're
We going
Today"

Do
We ever
Understand,
"Why we're
Striving to be
Bold everyday!"

The
Train

To be
An illumined
Being means
To be a
Spirit with
The freewill

To be
Moral means
We're
In the cradle
Of light always

Oh this
Train of
Thoughts,
Always
Keeps rolling
Toward the
Highest hope
Of all...

Where's
The Way

How
Do we
Reconcile
God's wrath with
Love and mercy
At the same time

How
Do we accept
Violence and wars
And His forgiveness
At the same time

How
Do we
Tell a child
Who sees our
Janus attitude
And we got
Audacity to ask
Him to be honest
At the same time!

Voice

Children
Kept marching
On a slippery
Terrain of the
Highland

They
Began their
Big climb
Even danger
Lurked behind
At all time

But
They didn't
Care and kept
Singing:

We're
Here to live
Well
Yes we're
Here to make
Some sense

We dare to
Go through
The darkness
For a while
To reach out
Highest peak of
The eternal light...

Power
Within

In this
Times of
Uncertainty
Let moral
Be the
Trait of him

In this
Times of
Insecurity
Must Insist
On a clarity of
His mission

Let him
Be an enlightened
Spirit
Let him
Drop all fallacies
And go for his
Genuine meaning.

Off The
Cuff

How do we
Apply common
Sense to wipe
Off the old trait
Full of harms

How do we
Erase lingering
Doubts and
Debates causing
Suffering too
Long

How do we
Rise above
The cacophony
And trash talks
To fulfill our
"Global Dream."

Inferno

What if
Life is
Nothing
More than
A brief
Hedonistic
Existence

What if
We're
Thrown into a
Deep shaft of
Despair and
There is
No escape to
Reset new life

What
If this habit of
War-mongering
Is holding us
As prisoners and
Who aren't willing
To escape!

Theme

Dwelling
Into the
Reality of
Recurring
Causes and
Consequences

Are them
Shaping our
Thoughts,
Words and
Deeds always

Is that
The way to
Ascend toward
The final end
Of our set
Journey or what

All is
Continuum
And exploding
Now and then and
Human is no
Exception to the
Ongoing play...

Sloths

Oh this
"Techno-magic"
Where nothing
More to attain
But be the jolly
Consumers... living
Off just day to day

People
Don't have
To sweat anymore
For robots and AI's
Shall do
All the chores

Rejoice
People
You are going to
Get free money and
Nothing to worry
For another job

Sorry,
'No freedom'
In return for
We shall not be the
Bonafide owners of
Our dignity at all...

Know
Thy
Future

Don't be
So afraid to
Walk the walk
When
Approaching
The temple of
Truth

Don't be
So ignorant,
When future is
Hanging between
Uncertainty and
Mass-extinction!

People,
Dear people
Time to leave the
Long slumber
Time to wake-up
And get to the
Purpose

Time
To hold hands
And fight head-on
Against the cascading
Dark time...

Acquiescence

History
Reminds us
Rich and powerful
Always
Ruled the world

Later,
By the pious
Servants who
Gained the upper
Hand
In the set godly
Game

There was a
Sunshine called,
"Age of
Enlightenment"
To change the
World for good

Though
An inspired
Historic event
Didn't change
The world as
Much and
We're
Still trying to
Redo it again. In
Our time...

A Point

To have
Courage means
To defend the
Dignity of others

To be
Ethical means
What it ought
To be

To be
Rational means
To discern
What is right and
What is not?

To be
Enlightened
Means to be
An integrated
Whole spirit

To be
Human means
To know the
Moral worth
In time...

Let's Roll

Why
Be hesitant
To take an action
And be triumphant
In the end

Why
Be afraid
To go beyond
Dogmas and
Quotidian
Mediocrity to
Seek,
"Who we're"

If we're
Born with a
Mandate of
Truth
Why
Run away
From it now

Why then
Are we
So helplessly
Begging for another
Forgiveness from Him...

Trust

Let us
Get to know
Our inner being
Where beauty and
Truth remains
For the good

Just take a
Glimpse inside,
"We're the
Rational souls"

Let
Us also know,
"We're bold
Only when we
Can validate our
Moral code"

Let the
Young admire
Their elders for
Handing over the
Helm on time."

Flashers

Hope
Always a glow
In the dark

Let
Neither
Guilt and nor
Grief control
The spirit

Love
What a spark
Between two
Waiting souls

Truth
What a
Conception to
Bring forth a
Rational closure
To the mind

Essence
What a silent
Light at the
Center of the
Ethical quest...

Conundrum

From
Failure to
Success and
More successes
There on
Such is the
Consequence of
His
Determined will

Being
Always a
Spinning wheel
Going from birth
To death and then
Flying off to eternity
For good

Human
What an
Obsession of
'Perfection"
Yet, afraid to
Express his
Ultimate intention...

Recurrences

Pseudo-
Beliefs,
Arrogance
And ignorance
Have been the
Recurring themes;
Halting human
Progress everyday

Modern
Time is no
Different as
Grey clouds
Keep passing
Now and then;
Threatening the
Glory of the
World everyday

Nukes,
Climate,
Violence
And constant
Bickering are
Killing our future
Everyday...

The
Flow

Each ego
Always a
Cause of
Some trouble

Each
Error has
Its price to
Pay in return

Each
Keeps mum
When fear is
Hanging over
The head

Each
In denial
When caught
Red-handed
On the spot

Each
Inching toward
Death every sec
And there is no
Surprise to report...

Identity

What is
Salvation?
Is it
A final
Judgment of
'Divine' or just
A fear-driven
Concern

What is
Worship?
Is it
Begging
To fulfill
Selfish wants;
Revealing
Our weakness

What is
God?
Is He just
A conceptual
Notion to
Survive or what

What is
Truth?
Is it just
Unknown to our
Consciousness or
Something else or
What!

Epiphany

All
Courage
Emanates
From the
Moral core of
Awakened being

That is
When his
'Freewill' and
Rational insight
Begins to take
Control

That is
When being
Becomes a
Cosmic meaning
In its true sense...

Attitude

Don't
Blame
Others for
Your failures

Don't
Fight others
For your fears

Don't
Miss to toss
The dice over
And again

Life
What a
Tossed coin
Having two
Sides:
"Good and
Evil" printed
In human psyche
As always...

Voices

I hear
Voices from
Faraway places
To be free of
Any blind belief

I hear
Voices from the
Distance galaxies
Asking to seek
Truth beyond
Always

I hear
Voices from
My spirit
Demanding to
Keep the journey
Rolling with
Confidence and
Determined Will...

Why
Exists

Being
What a sum
Total of reality
Who's inevitably
Measured by
The time between
Birth and death

Being
What a gift of
Creativity to
Streamline his
Very essence
In this world of
Falsity and
Pseudo-worship
From beginning to
The very end

Being
What a magic
Living light
Let him
Get off the
State of violence,
Ignorance and
Arrogance to gain
A right purpose
To his noble birth...

Outcome

Hell and
Heaven
(H & H)
Divided equal
For every being
At the time of
Birth

As life
Evolves,
Pot pouri of
Experiences
Define the
Consequence
Alright

As the
Pendulum
H & H
Swings so does
Consequential
Destiny of him/her
In the end...

Widening
Circles

Existence
But an ever
Widening circles
Of challenges and
Struggles while
Walking through
His time

Human
Never gets
To know the real
Within so well
And he's lost
Always in the
Storm

Against
Such anguish,
He wonders,
"What's
The purpose of
Soul's journeying
Through this
Temporal to eternal,
After all!"

Wake-up

This is the
Time to
Resurrect the
"Global Spirit"

This the
Chance to be
The winners of
Our set mission

Let us not
Be afraid to
Live with
Courage and
Freewill to
Make it right

There
Ain't time left
To complain
There
Ain't time left
To neglect
There
Ain't time left
To regret...

Conscious Universe

Let it be
Understood
All things are
Contextual in
This holistic
Universe

All events
And lives are
Interconnected
And communicates
With one another
In this conscious
Reality indeed

Let it be
Also grasped,
Intelligent life
Exists to clarify
The riddles and
Contradictions
Between the soul and
The mighty universe...

First Step

To be
Enlightened
Is to be a kind
Spirit

A spirit
Powered by
Rational goodwill
And moral genius

That is the
First step
Toward
Making of a
'Perfect Being"

That is the
Right direction
To roll from this
Point on

That is the
Right track to
Fly fearlessly from
Birth to death with
Dignity and grace....

In the
21st

Children
Kept asking,
"Why our
World is plagued
With so much
Insecurity and many
Million deaths?"

"Why
We've been
Trapped into this
Chaos and greed
For a very long?"

Young also
Questioning,
"Why there is
So much chaos in
Their elder's world?"

Avoir

Let
Us learn to
Say,
"Goodbye"
To the world
With a big smile"

Let us be
Bold to declare,
"I've always
Welcomed this
Great journey
That molded my
Point of view"

Let us
Also know,
"It doesn't
Matter if we're
Either right or
Wrong, but our
Efforts must be
Sincere all the way"

That's the
Only thought
We must leave
Behind and continue
The journey beyond...

Recent Books by J.J. Bhatt

(Available from Amazon)

HUMAN ENDEAVOR: Essence & Mission/ a Call for
Global Awakening, (2011)

ROLLING SPIRITS: Being Becoming /a Trilogy, (2012)

ODYSSEY OF THE DAMNED: *A Revolving Destiny,* (2013).

PARISHRAM: Journey of the Human Spirits, (2014).

TRIUMPH OF THE BOLD: A Poetic Reality, (2015).

THEATER OF WISDOM, *(2016).*

MAGNIFICENT QUEST: Life, Death & Eternity, (2016)

ESSENCE OF INDIA: A Comprehensive Perspective, (2016).

ESSENCE OF CHINA: Challenges & Possibilities, (2016).

BEING & MORAL PERSUASION: A Bolt of Inspiration, (2017).

REFELCTIONS, RECOLLECTIONS & EXPRESSIONS, (2018).

ONE, TWO, THREE... ETERNITY: *A Poetic Odyssey,(* 2018).

INDIA: Journey of Enlightenment (2019.)

SPINNING MIND, SPINNING TIME: *C'est la vie* (2019).Book 1.

MEDITATION ON HOLY TRINITY *(2019), Book 2.*

ENLIGHTENMENT: *Fiat lux* (2019), Book 3.

BEING IN THE CONTEXTUAL ORBIT: *Rhythm, Melody & Meaning* (2019)

QUINTESSENCE: *Thought & Action* (2019)

THE WILL TO ASCENT: *Power of Boldness & Genius* (2019)

RIDE ON A SPINNING WHEEL: *Existence Introspected,*   (2020a)

A FLASH OF LIGHT: *Splendors, Perplexities & Riddles* (2020b)

ON A ZIG ZAG TRAIL: *The Flow of Life* (2020c).

UNBOUNDED: *An Inner Sense of Destiny* (2020d).

REVERBERATIONS: The *Cosmic Pulse* (2020e).

LIGHT & DARK: *Dialogue and Meaning* (2021a).

ROLLING REALITY: *Being in flux (2021b).*

FORMAL SPLENDOR: *The Inner Rigor (2021c)*

TEMPORAL TO ETERNAL*: A Renewed Expedition (2021d)*

TRAILBLAZERS: The Spears of Courage (2021e)

■ ι

JAGDISH   J. BHATT, PhD brings 45 years of academic experience including the post-doctorate scientist at Stanford University, CA and authorship of numerous publications including 37 books which cover the scientific and the literary fields.